Enriqué Speaks with His Hands

Hilton Publishing Company
Chicago, IL

Direct all correspondence to:
Hilton Publishing Company
1630 45th Street, Suite 103
Munster, IN 46321
219-922-4868
www.hiltonpub.com

ISBN-13: 978-0-9800649-3-3

Library of Congress Cataloging-in-Publication Data

Fudge, Benjamin.
  Enriqué speaks with his hands / written by Benjamin Fudge ; [illustrator, Tim Edmonson].
    p. cm.
  Summary: A young deaf boy feels isolated and misunderstood until he is taken to a neighboring village where he meets other deaf children and discovers sign language.
    ISBN 978-0-9800649-3-3
    [1. Deaf--Fiction. 2. People with disabilities–Fiction. 3. Sign language–Fiction.] I. Edmonson, Tim, ill. II. Title.
    PZ7.F942En 2008
    [E]–dc22
                                                                    2007051957

Printed and bound in Mexico

Enriqué Speaks with His Hands

By Benjamin Fudge

Illustrated by Tim Edmonson

Hilton Publishing Company • Chicago Illinois

The early morning light shone through the trees and into the room as Mama stood up from the bed.

She moved quietly across the small one room house past the curtain hanging in the middle of the room and into the kitchen.

As she added some twigs to the fire, Mama thought, "Today will be the day. Today the new baby will come."

Soon Rosa and Corina came into the kitchen to get their breakfast.

"Mama, you put sugar in the avina," Rosa giggled, with happy surprise, while Corina looked on. "Yes," said Mama. "Today is going to be a special day. Today we will have a new baby."

The girls finished eating and put on their uniforms and left for school.

Mama began cleaning the house and the front yard. There was much to be done, to prepare for the arrival of the new baby.

Mama worked hard sweeping and mopping. She cleaned the dishes and placed them aside. Mama was very worried about the new baby, but she did not know why. This time felt different from the arrival of Corina or Rosa.

Later that day, he was born.

"Your little brother is here," Mama told the girls. "His name is Enriqué. We now have a boy. He is our special one!"

Enriqué was a beautiful baby with dark curly hair and skin the color of almonds; and Mama and the girls were happy.

But deep inside, Mama knew that something was not right.

One day, when little Enriqué was sleeping, the rain came. The sky turned dark. The wind blew hard.

Suddenly there was a crash of thunder. Mama jumped. The girls screamed. Baby Enriqué did not cry.

Mama looked at him and felt the coldness come into her . . . for now Mama knew. Baby Enriqué could not hear.

As little Enriqué grew, his world was dark with no sound.

Mama loved him, but did not know how to help him.

His sisters loved him, but they did not understand what was wrong with Enriqué.

Enriqué knew he was different.

When he tried to play with the other children in the village, they would look at him and laugh. Sometimes they would push him or hit him or throw stones at him.

Even the other mamas and papas in the village would point at him and say things.

He could not hear them, but he felt their words: "That's Enriqué–the strange one!"

Enriqué felt alone and sad.

One day when he was older, a stranger came to the village.

This was a stranger like no one they had ever seen before.
She was tall, and her skin was white, and she had red hair–
lots of red hair.

Enriqué hid behind Mama as the stranger talked with her. Mama looked at Enriqué. The stranger looked at him, too.

But when she looked at him, the stranger smiled and it was different from the smiles of the villagers.

Her smile made Enriqué smile inside—and he felt something he had never felt before, something he did not understand, but it felt good.

Mama and the white lady with the big red hair talked for a long time, while Enriqué watched.

At last the white lady waved good-bye and walked to her van.

Enriqué watched her leave and he felt sad to see her go.

Many days went by until early one morning Mama woke
Enriqué.

She helped him wash and dress in his best clothes. Then they
sat and waited. Mama kept looking out the door.

Then they saw something at the end of their road—it was the
van of the white lady with the big red hair!

Once the van stopped Mama and Enriqué climbed inside.

The lady with the red hair greeted Mama and Enriqué with a huge smile.

But, Enriqué was scared. They had never done anything like this before.

They drove to the next village and stopped at the church hall.

Enriqué looked in fear as he saw there were many boys and girls there. He was afraid they would be mean to him like the children in his village.

But then, Enriqué saw something else—all of these children were moving their hands in some kind of special way. As Enriqué watched, he knew in his heart that they were like him. They were deaf.

The lady with the big red hair had some friends with her and he saw that they were talking with their hands, like the children.

The lady and her friends moved the children into groups and they began their work.

That day Enriqué learned to say many things with his hands.
He learned "Mama" and "Papa."
He learned "dog" and "food."
He learned "water" and "bed."

And he learned to say, "I love you."

Mama was learning the word signs, too, and when Enriqué
signed, "I love you" to Mama, she was so happy she cried.

The lady with the big red hair started coming every week and took Mama and Enriqué to the village. Enriqué learned more and more.

One day when the lady came, he greeted her with words from his hands. She talked back to him with her hands. And he understood.

As the weeks went by the darkness inside him changed to light.

The children saw how Enriqué grew and how he had learned. Now when they pointed, they smiled and said, "That's Enriqué–the special one!"

Enriqué smiled back. He felt good inside.

Like Enriqué, you also can learn sign language. You can begin by learning the alphabet shown on the next page.

a   b   c   d   e   f   g

h   i   j   k   l   m

 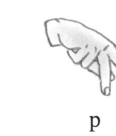 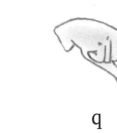  

n   o   p   q   r   s

t   u   v   w   x   y   z

To Robin, Susan, family, and friends at Elderberry.
With appreciation and love.

Author's Note

While this story is a work of fiction, it is based on a real Enriqué and a real group of people who are bringing language and hope to deaf children. My wife, daughter and I met Enriqué on a visit to Honduras in March 2003, and my life was touched forever.

To find out more about the real white lady with big red hair and the children she serves in rural villages of Honduras, go to: www.Signsoflove.org or write: Signs of Love / Señas de Amor P.O. Box 3852, Apple Valley, CA 92307.